LITTLE TOOT
THROUGH
THE GOLDEN GATE

LITTLE TOOT

THROUGH THE GOLDEN GATE

HARDIE GRAMATKY

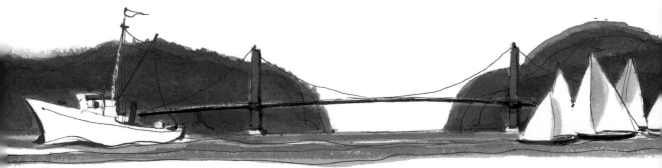

G. P. Putnam's Sons   New York

Through the Golden Gate came
Little Toot puffing big, black
smoke balls. The little tugboat
had journeyed a long way over
rough seas. Now before him lay a
beautiful bay.

It was a bay filled with boats. Not that there is anything unusual about a bay filled with boats, but these boats were different. They were joyful and gay. Little Toot's eyes opened wide.

Sailboats frolicked and played. They
were as carefree as the brisk ocean breeze.
Ferryboats blasted their deep-throated
whistles and pushed their bows boldly
into the crisp, choppy waves. Crab boats
cavorted about like circus clowns.

Little Toot looked himself over
fore and aft. He wondered what it
would be like to be a sailboat . . .
to be joyful, so easy in the breeze,
so full of life. He quickly blew the
soot off his smokestack. He gave a
flip to the flag on his stern. Then
with a cheerful toot on his whistle
he set out to join in the fun.

"Perhaps I could be a sailboat,"
he thought hopefully.

"I could be a ferryboat, too.

"I might even be a crab boat . . .
if I chose to be."

Of one thing Little Toot was certain.
This was an exciting new world.
This was a world filled with fun.

Little Toot looked around him.
Along the waterfront were docked
ships from all over the world.
High above the waterfront loomed
the hills of the city. Tall buildings
crowned the tops of the hills,
while streets ran down like silver
ribbons tying the hills to the bay.

On the hills were cheerful-looking houses. Their tall windows, like large glistening eyes, watched out over this beautiful world.

A fat, jolly cable car came bumping and thumping down the hill. It was loaded to overflowing with a group of boys and girls.

Excitedly the boys and girls piled
off at the Embarcadero, no doubt
to watch the ships unload. They

watched for a long time. But the
more they watched, the sadder
they became, and perhaps for a
good reason, too. Barrels of
pickles, pork, and pigs' feet were
unloaded all over the dock. This
was not at all the cargo the boys
and girls had hoped to find, but
that's all the cargo there was.

Silently, the boys and girls
trudged sadly back up the hill.

"Why aren't those boys and girls
happy . . . like the sailboats?"
thought Little Toot. "Sailboats
enjoy life and have fun."

Suddenly, the thought of fun sent
Little Toot scurrying back to the
sailboats.

He threw himself into being a frolicking sailboat. He skimmed over the water with ease. He drifted carefree as the birds overhead. He tacked into the wind with great vigor. Then he came about as freely as a swan.

But alas! Little Toot came about
much too freely . . . and ran
smack into a bulky old freighter.

It was the Saucy Sal from Sausalito, a gloomy old boat at best. The Saucy Sal had been battered about by ocean waves and was in no mood for the antics of a playful little tugboat. "Tugboats are built for towing," grumbled the Saucy Sal. "Be the tugboat you were meant to be."

But Little Toot didn't want
to be a tugboat. He wanted to
be a ferryboat instead. *Ferryboats
lead exciting lives.* Little Toot
was sure. He blew a deep-throated
toot on his whistle and pushed
his bow boldly into the crisp,
choppy waves.

He might even have been taken
for a ferryboat had he not been
caught up in the waves. They
were too much for Little Toot. In
the confusion of not knowing
which way to go he ran directly
across a ferryboat's bow. It was an
awful thing to do. To avoid
running into the little tugboat, the
old boats ran afoul of each other.

"What a fine crab boat you could be." A voice surprised him from behind. Little Toot looked around and saw a grinning crab boat. "But I'm not a crab boat," protested the little tugboat politely. "You could be a great crab boat, if you tried. It's a lot of fun," replied all the crab boats together. "Come with us and you'll see."

Little Toot chugged off happily
with his new friends.

But alas! Hunting crabs was not quite the fun Little Toot had hoped for. Not at all! Instead of the fun he was to have hunting crabs, the crabs had more fun hunting him.

The crab boats were furious because they had caught no crabs, so they took out their anger on Little Toot. "You're not a crab boat!" they cried. "You're not a sailboat! You're not a ferryboat either! You're a *nothing!*"

"A *nothing!*" breathed Little Toot. The little tugboat was chilled and frightened. "A nothing is a horrible thing to be."

A strange-looking cloud rolled into the cloudless sky. It grew into a great white ghost as it moved quietly over the city. It devoured buildings and houses as it came.

Then it crept down the hills to the bay, and in no time at all its long arms reached out to Little Toot.

Cool, gentle fingers caught him up
in a mist and he was swallowed up
in a monstrous fog.

The fog was so dense that Little
Toot could see nothing. There was
nothing in front of him. Nothing
behind him. Nothing on either
side. Frantically, the little tugboat
looked around to find himself. *He
wasn't there at all!* "I *am*
nothing!" sobbed Little Toot.
"The crab boats were right. I am
nothing at all!"

Things were pretty hopeless.
Little Toot floated about like
nothing in a nothingness world.
After what seemed a million years
. . . perhaps an hour or so . . . the
fog began to lift. Little Toot
thought he saw the tip of his nose.
Then he saw the visor of his cap.
Quickly, he looked back over his
shoulder . . . *and there he saw
himself again!*

"I am *me!*" cried Little Toot. "I'm not nothing. I am me . . . and I am a tugboat!"

Standing next to Little Toot was the Saucy Sal from Sausalito. The old freighter had run out of steam in the fog and was waiting to be towed into shore.

"I'll tow you!" tooted Little Toot. *"I'm* a tugboat! I am the tugboat I was meant to be, and I can tow a boat as well as my father can."

The Saucy Sal had her doubts,
but she threw the little tugboat
a line.

Little Toot began to tow. He towed with all his might. He towed until he was green in the face, but the Saucy Sal never budged. The old boat stood there big and bulky and loaded to her top deck with cargo. Not in the least discouraged, Little Toot tugged harder than ever. His little engine roared. Fire and smoke shot out of his smokestack like fireworks. Still he could not move the old freighter.

Little Toot's eyes filled with tears.
He was about to give up when
with one last great tug he felt the
Saucy Sal slide forward. Another
enormous tug, and the old
freighter was well under way.
Little Toot towed as he had never
towed before. It may be he was
getting much stronger.

Or it may have been the extra
boost he got from the crab boats
back on the stern.

Little Toot and the freighter made
a wide circle, then pulled up
alongside the Embarcadero. No
one was there to greet them. The
boys and girls had been down to
the dock again, but when they
saw the Saucy Sal, they had given
up hope entirely. "More pickles,
pork, and pigs' feet," someone said
as they started back up the hill.

But wait!

This time some fine-looking crates were unloaded onto the dock. On the crates were colorful labels that the boys and girls knew well. "The musical instruments we sent for!" they shouted excitedly. "Our ship has come in at last!"

The crates were quickly opened. There to everyone's delight were shiny brass horns, big bass drums, guitars, tubas, trumpets, and sliding trombones. All got the instruments they had wanted, and all were overcome with joy.

The joy on their faces dazzled Little Toot. "Those boys and girls are as happy as sailboats now," observed Little Toot. "None of us is a *nothing* anymore!"

It was true. Bands played.
Sailboats sailed. Ferryboats
ferried. Crab boats crabbed. And
Little Toot tugged. They all did
what each did best. It was the
best of all possible worlds.

When time came for Little Toot
to go home, he tooted a
cheerful farewell on his whistle.
Someone picked up the gay note
on a piccolo, another rolled it
off on a drum. Sea gulls fluttered
about the little tugboat as he
chugged out through the beautiful
Golden Gate.

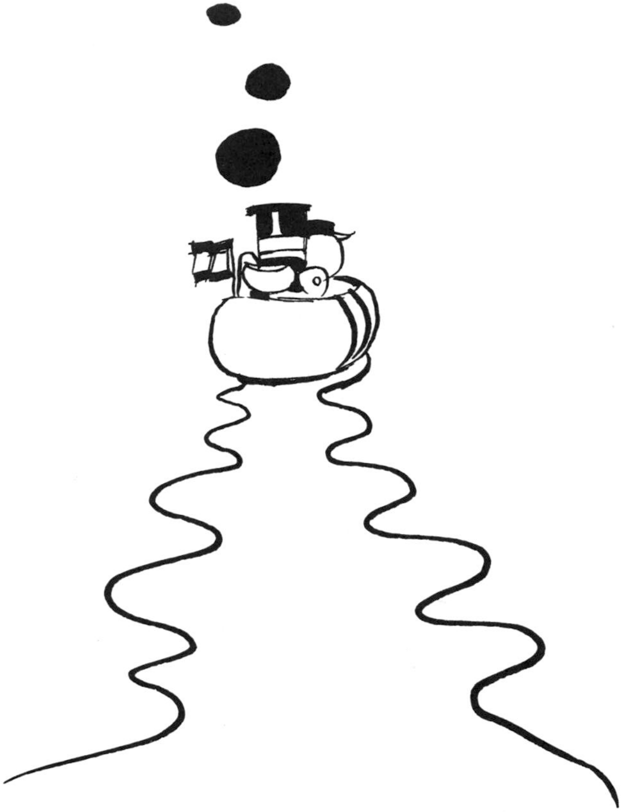

The Author

HARDIE GRAMATKY is the author-illustrator of the children's classic, *Little Toot*. For a third of a century children have delighted in the adventures of the pixie-ish tugboat. Three sequels have told of the further adventures of Little Toot, while eight other books for children have come from the author's colorful imagination. Mr. Gramatky is famous for his paintings and is the winner of more than forty major awards for watercolors.